MONSTER CRUISE!

Adapted by
Jesse Burton

Illustrated by
Adam Devaney

Simon Spotlight
New York London Toronto Sydney New Delhi

SIMON SPOTLIGHT
An imprint of Simon & Schuster Children's Publishing Division
1230 Avenue of the Americas, New York, New York 10020
This Simon Spotlight edition June 2018

For information about special discounts for bulk purchases, please contact Simon & Schuster Special Sales at
1-866-506-1949 or business@simonandschuster.com.
Manufactured in the United States of America 0418 LAK
2 4 6 8 10 9 7 5 3 1
ISBN 978-1-5344-1768-7
ISBN 978-1-5344-1769-4 (eBook)

Mavis didn't know what to do. Even though Hotel Transylvania ran smoothly, it was a lot of work. So she and her father never had time for their family and friends..

"Do you need some family time? Are you a monster? Then you need a vacation! A monster vacation!" proclaimed an announcer on a television commercial.

And in that moment Mavis knew *exactly* what Drac and his pack needed: a vacation.

It wasn't just any vacation. It was a once-in-a-lifetime cruise for monsters that started in the legendary Bermuda Triangle and sailed to the lost city of Atlantis. Drac and his friends were amazed by the cruise ship. Monsters from all over the world boarded alongside the Drac Pack.

Drac loved Mavis's sweet surprise. He adored spending time with his family and friends and couldn't wait to see what adventures were in store for them. Exotic locations? Gourmet dining? Nonstop entertainment? Drac was ready for whatever came his way.

But he was not ready for what happened when Ericka, the ship's captain, introduced herself to the travelers. One look at her, and Drac Zinged! He had only Zinged once before—with Mavis's mother. *Was it even possible to Zing twice?*

"Doobie-day-shu-la eh koobie. Ali-booboo," said Drac when he met Ericka, who didn't know what to make of Drac's silly babbling.

So she replied, "Ali-booboo to you" and went on her way.

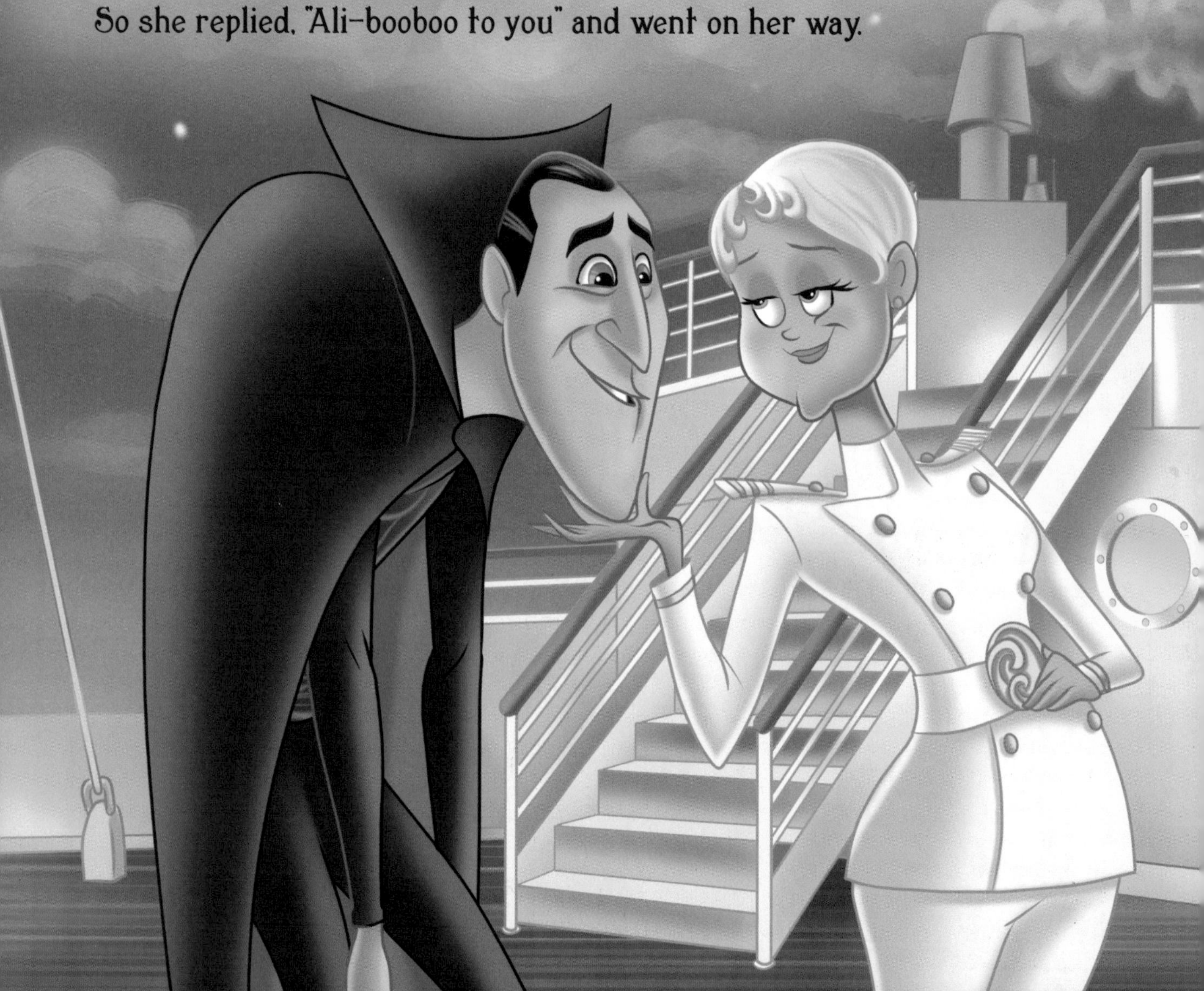

After another goofy encounter with Ericka, Drac told his friends what was going on. It felt good to Zing again. But he also worried about Mavis. She, Johnny, and Dennis were his family. He had to be there for them. Everything else was a distraction.

"Family family, fun fun," Drac reminded himself.

The Drac Pack was excited for him. They loved seeing Drac so happy.
"Make some small talk," encouraged Murray.
"Ask her if she likes coffins," said Griffin.
"Compliment her: Your neck looks delicious," suggested Frank.

Just then Captain Ericka came walking by. Drac seized the moment.

"Your delicious neck wrappings are in the nice coffin would you like to see my parts?" asked a hopelessly tongue-tied Drac.

That night Drac snuck away to meet Ericka. At dinner she pretended to be interested in him so she could feed him garlic-laced guacamole. She hoped it would do him in.

PWEEEEEEEEEEEEEEEEEPH! Instead of dying, he tooted! Drac was so embarrassed and nervous. He admitted that this was his first date since his wife died, and he had a lot on his mind.

"The past stays with us. But we make our own future," said Drac.

This surprised Ericka. She never thought she'd relate to a monster like Drac. Plotting against monsters made it hard for her to think about the future.

The night got worse. Drac had forgotten that he had offered to babysit Dennis. When an angry Mavis arrived at the restaurant, Drac told her it was just a business meeting. His date did not end well.

Soon enough, the ship arrived at Atlantis, their final destination. The monsters were invited to explore the lost city's sights. They were also promised a huge celebration. All the monsters were having a great time.

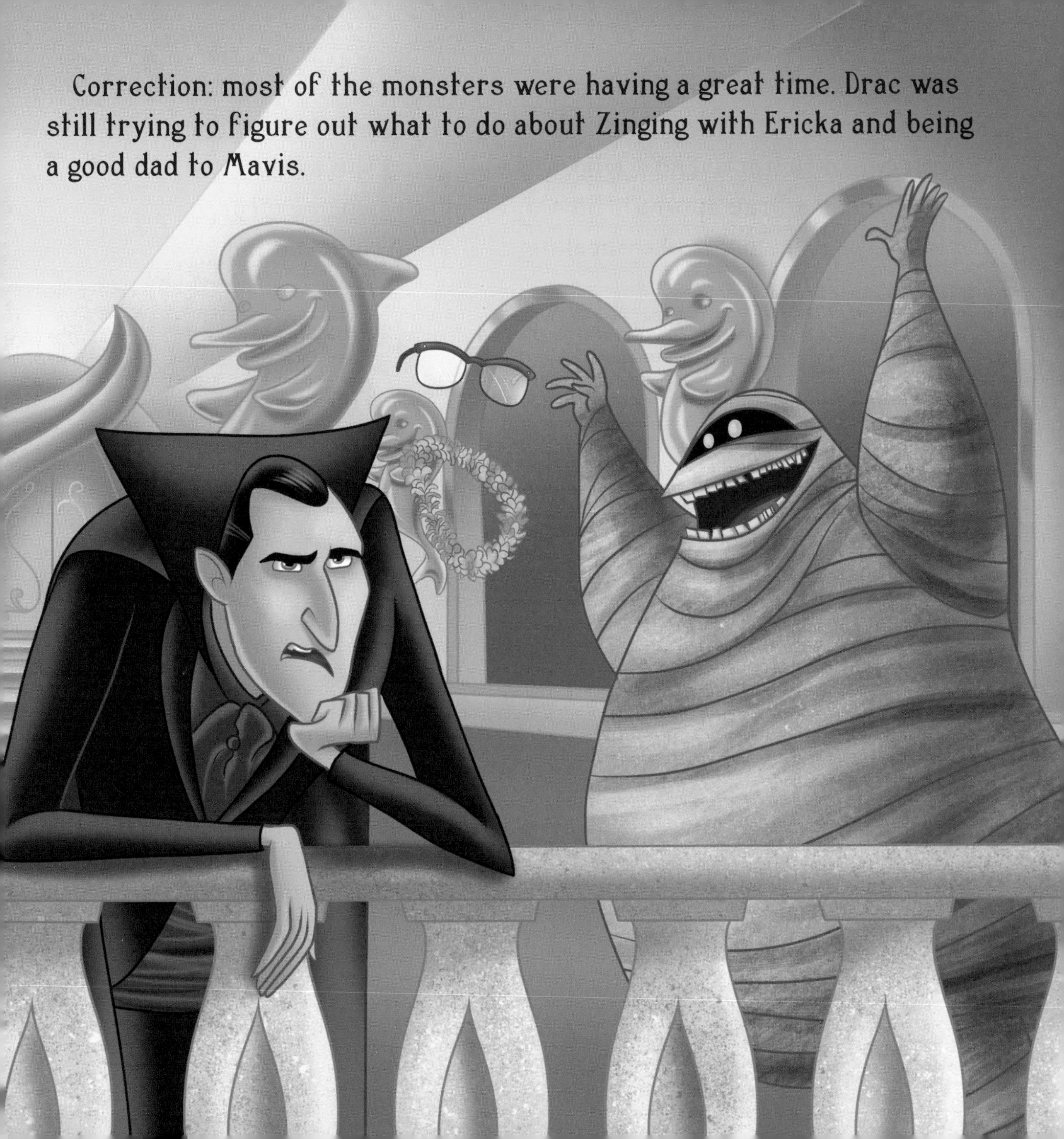

Correction: most of the monsters were having a great time. Drac was still trying to figure out what to do about Zinging with Ericka and being a good dad to Mavis.

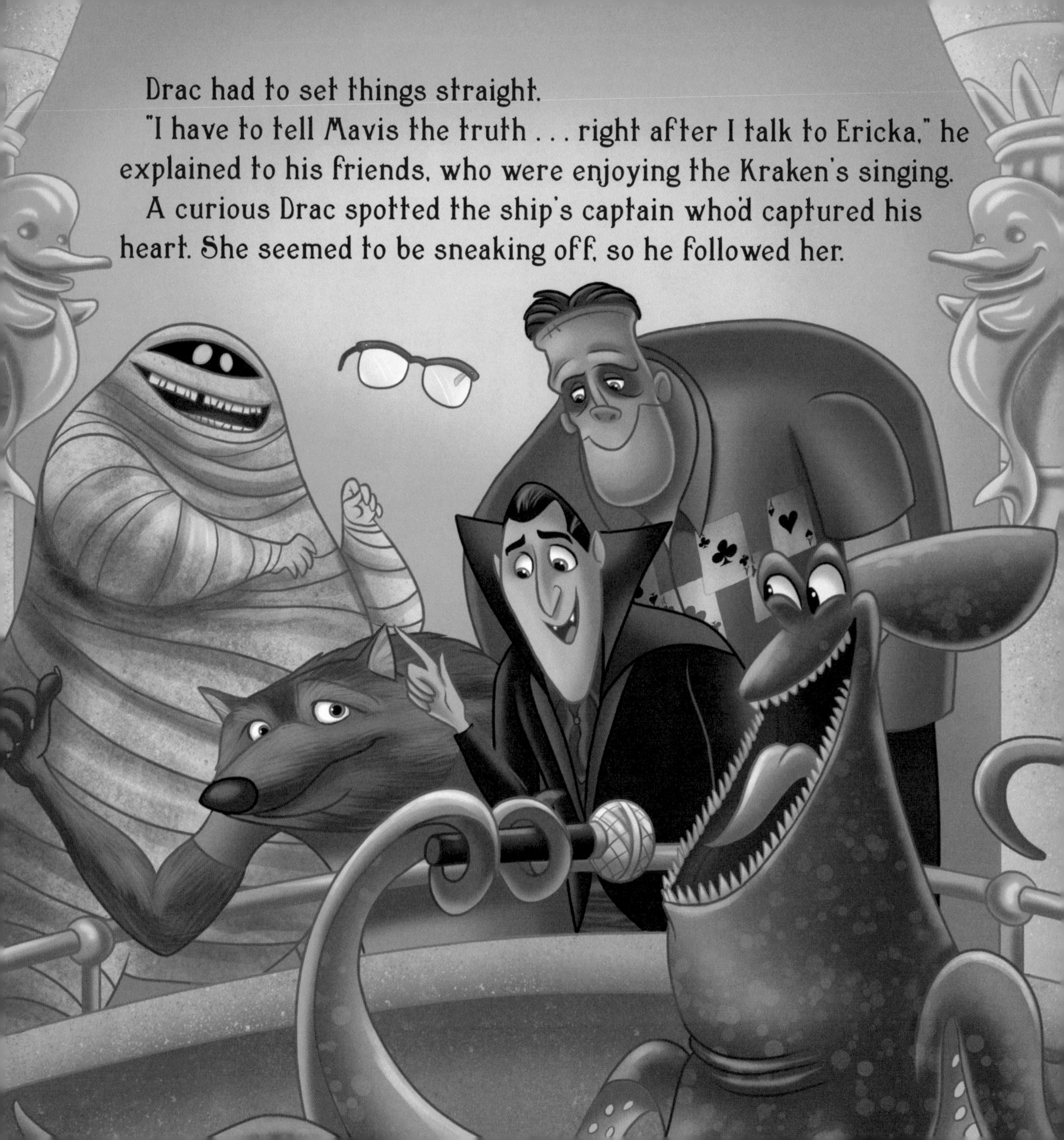

Drac had to set things straight.

"I have to tell Mavis the truth . . . right after I talk to Ericka," he explained to his friends, who were enjoying the Kraken's singing.

A curious Drac spotted the ship's captain who'd captured his heart. She seemed to be sneaking off, so he followed her.

Ericka crept down a staircase and entered a passageway toward an underground pool. She dove into the water. Drac followed her.

Erika ended up in a throne room. She was so focused on her mission that she didn't even hear Drac arrive. She just stared at the stone figure holding a device.

As she took a step forward, an ax flew out of the wall. Luckily, Drac grabbed the ax before it struck Ericka.

"You saved my life? I can't believe you would do that for a human," said Ericka.

"Humans, monsters, what's the difference?" said Drac.

Ericka didn't believe Drac. So she tested him. She told him she was there to reclaim a family heirloom. Every step Ericka took set off a new booby trap! And each time Drac saved Ericka from flying axes, arrows, and darts.

"That was incredible!" said Ericka.

"Don't you want your crystal ball thingy?" asked Drac.

Ericka had completely forgotten about the device. She hesitated at first, then finally grabbed it. As soon as she did, the room started to collapse. Drac scooped up Ericka and dived back into the pool. He saved her again.

But before Drac and Ericka could catch their breath, Mavis confronted the couple. She'd been following them. Seeing her father impaled with all the axes, arrows, and darts convinced Mavis that Ericka was up to no good.

"What are you doing to my father?" yelled Mavis.

Drac finally admitted that he had Zinged with Ericka. This surprised Mavis and Ericka.

"I could never be with a monster," said Ericka as she ran away.

At the big Atlantis celebration Johnny helped Mavis realize that Drac deserved to be happy, just like they were. She encouraged her father to follow his destiny and talk with Ericka. Drac went looking for Ericka.

He was shocked to find her with his sworn enemy—and her grandfather—Van Helsing! The trip to Atlantis? The mysterious device? It was a trap to destroy the monsters. Drac was devastated.

So was Ericka. She was falling for Drac. She loved how sweet he was with his family and friends. She was awed that he would risk his life to save hers over and over again.

Johnny helped save the day too. Thanks to his DJ skills, he played the happiest song he knew to calm the Kraken. Everyone at the party, even Van Helsing and the Kraken, started to dance!

Mavis could not be happier for her dad. He had his family, friends, and someone to Zing who Zinged him back! What more could he need?

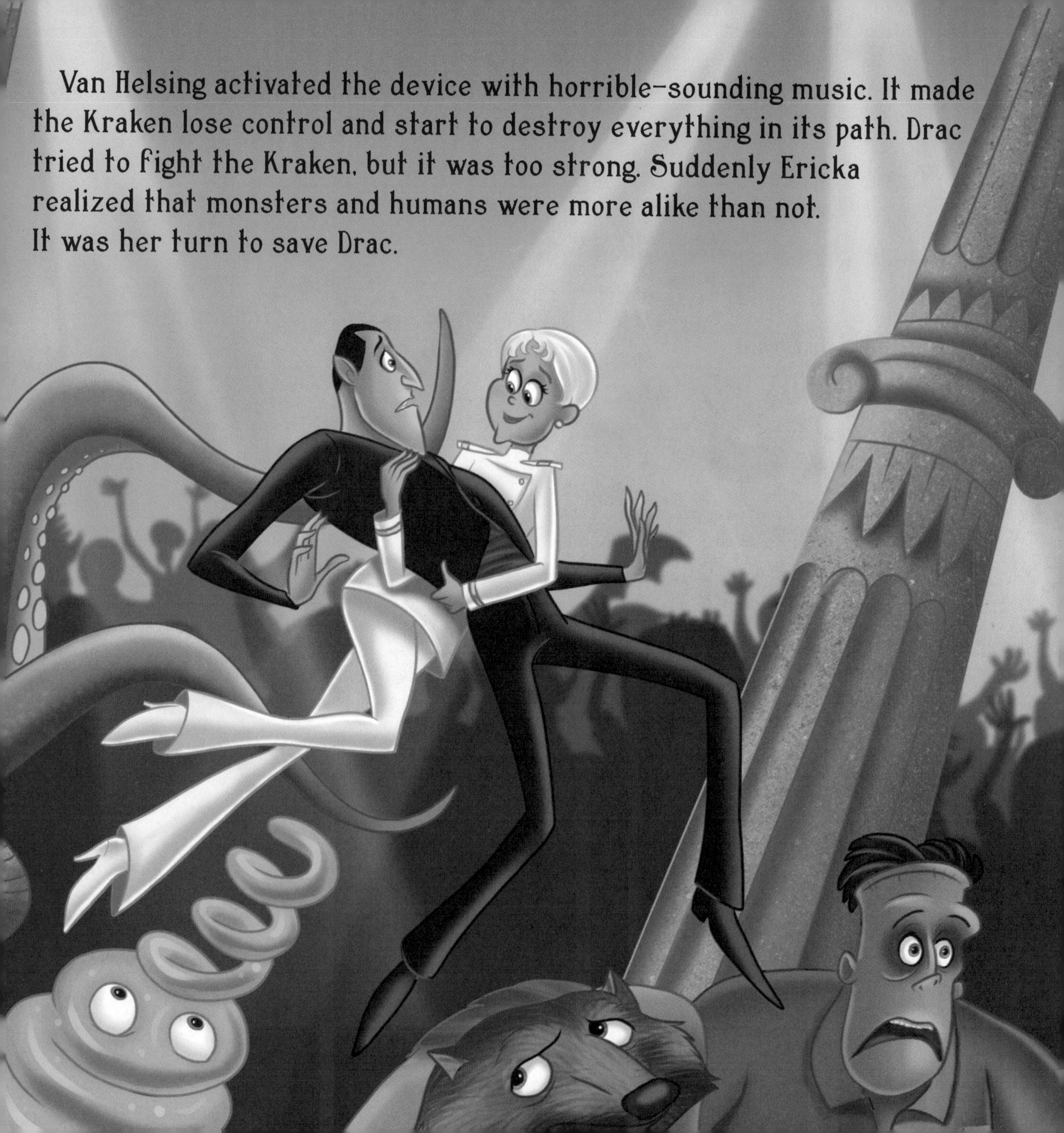

Van Helsing activated the device with horrible-sounding music. It made the Kraken lose control and start to destroy everything in its path. Drac tried to fight the Kraken, but it was too strong. Suddenly Ericka realized that monsters and humans were more alike than not. It was her turn to save Drac.